Acting Edition

I0591775

Where We Stand

by Donnetta Lavinia Grays

FOR PRODUCTION INQUIRIES

UNITED STATES AND CANADA
info@concordtheatricals.com
1-866-979-0447

UNITED KINGDOM AND EUROPE
licensing@concordtheatricals.co.uk
020-7054-7298

Each title is subject to availability from Concord Theatricals Corp.,
depending upon country of performance. Please be aware that
WHERE WE STAND may not be licensed by Concord Theatricals Corp.
in your territory. Professional and amateur producers should contact
the nearest Concord Theatricals Corp. office or licensing partner to
verify availability.

No one shall make any changes in this title(s) for the purpose of production. No part of this book may be reproduced, stored in a retrieval system, scanned, uploaded, or transmitted in any form, by any means, now known or yet to be invented, including mechanical, electronic, digital, photocopying, recording, videotaping, or otherwise, without the prior written permission of the publisher. No one shall share this title(s), or any part of this title(s), through any social media or file hosting websites.

For all inquiries regarding motion picture, television, online/digital and other media rights, please contact Concord Theatricals Corp.

THIRD-PARTY MATERIALS USE NOTE

Licensees are solely responsible for obtaining formal written permission from copyright owners to use copyrighted third-party materials (e.g., incidental music not provided in connection with a performance license, artworks, logos) in the performance of this play and are strongly cautioned to do so. If no such permission is obtained by the licensee, then the licensee must use only original materials and materials that the licensee owns and controls. Licensees are solely responsible and liable for clearances of all third-party copyrighted materials, and shall indemnify the copyright owners of the play(s) and their licensing agent, Concord Theatricals Corp., against any costs, expenses, losses and liabilities arising from the use of such copyrighted third-party materials by licensees. For music, please contact the appropriate music licensing authority in your territory for the rights to any incidental music not provided in connection with a performance license.

IMPORTANT BILLING AND CREDIT REQUIREMENTS

If you have obtained performance rights to this title, please refer to your licensing agreement for important billing and credit requirements.

WHERE WE STAND was originally commissioned by The Public Theater's Mobile Unit (Stephanie Ybarra, Director of Special Artistic Projects and The Mobile Unit). The play received a workshop through The Public Theater's Brooklyn College Research Residency August 7th – 17th 2018. David Ryan Smith was the performer. Tamilla Woodard directed. The piece was presented as part of the 2018 Prelude Festival October 6th 2018. Donnetta Lavinia Grays was the performer. The play continued development at SPACE on Ryder Farm where Donnetta was a Working Farm Resident Playwright. *Where We Stand* received further development at The New Harmony Project's Spring Conference May 20th – June 2nd 2019 where Donnetta was a Writer in Full Development. Brian D. Coats and Stacey Karen Robinson were the performers. Tamilla Woodard directed. *Where We Stand* received its world premiere with a co-production between WP Theater (Lisa McNulty, Artistic Director) in New York and Baltimore Center Stage (Stephanie Ybarra, Artistic Director) Spring 2020 under Tamilla Woodard's direction. Nehemiah Luckett served as both Music Dramaturg and Music Director. Norman Anthony Small served as Production Stage Manager. Donnetta Lavinia Grays and David Ryan Smith rotated performances. Donnetta Lavinia Grays gave the opening night performance.

CHARACTERS

MAN
STRANGER
TOWNSPERSON
TOWNSPERSON (MIDDLE-AGED MAN)
TOWNSPERSON (OLD WOMAN)
TOWNSPERSON (DOC. HUMPHREY)
TOWNSPERSON ('LITTLE HORNS' LADY)
TOWNSPERSON (DAVEY)
TOWNSPERSON (ORCHARD LADY)

SETTING

We are where we are. The space is as unique and is as simple as the space in which we are gathered. And wherever we are gathered, we are at this town's center. We are who we are. The people are as multifaceted as the people who have gathered in this space. And whoever is gathered, we are the people who make up this town.

TIME

The time is now. And whenever the time is,
we are both at the end of our journey and at its very beginning.

PERFORMANCE NOTES

Casting

This is a solo performance piece. **MAN** is a name given solely due to the creative limitations of the writer. **MAN** should be played by any African-American body with a body. Play **MAN** with *your* body in *your* complete self. Do not play the character of a masculine gendered person if that is not who you are. The play requires your*self* to be the *self* that embodies this story. Invite your unique YOU-ness to this space and make no alterations or adjustments toward the idea of gender beyond the situation of the play. Think of **MAN** as short for the 'EVERYMAN' and of yourself as its best representation. What is required is that you come into the space with honesty, humility and an astounding level of vulnerability, generosity and virtuosity.

Throughout the piece there are named townspeople (i.e Sarah, Davey, Doc Humphrey etc.). These are audience members meant to be cast by the **MAN** in real time. They aren't required to do anything more than be present as the **MAN** inhabits their body/character in the storytelling. Others are nameless, but their language is quoted. They require the same level of real time audience casting and physical/vocal embodiment by the **MAN**.

For the purposes of depicting accurate gender expressions, please feel free to alter any pronouns – **NOT character names or ANY other aspects of the text** – to fit the performer's gender expression and their relationship to the other characters in the piece.

EXAMPLE: *Yes! And I took that scythe. Like to have one hand 'round ya partner. Small of **her** back tucked deep in the crux of your elbow.*

Her may be altered in this line to meet the performer where they are.

Language

The entire piece has an internal rhythm. Outside of the songs the whole event should feel lyrical in nature. Follow the rhyme – *and* when it is broken – as a roadmap to the storytelling and to inform the drive of the piece. Think of Jazz, Blues, Gospel, Spoken Word and American Musical Theater traditions for guidance. Mind the punctuation. Non-italicized language in parenthesis () should be spoken. The spoken language is meant to meld into the singing flawlessly with no rest given between their merger. Spacing should be minded as a shift in thought or intention. *Italics* indicate a lift in the language. Songs are in all caps. Spoken sections within songs are always in tempo.

Singing

If you are not a singer, that's okay. The songs are meant to live closer to your speaking voice. So, bring your voice to the piece. Your voice is important and is exactly where it should be. Use it as your baseline for singing. Sing in the key that works most naturally for you without pushing. The singing is meant to meld into the spoken language flawlessly with no rest given between their merger.

Set/Staging

The piece demands equity; a democracy of space not usually attended to in theater. We are not 'audience' and 'performer' in a hierarchal set up. We are a community. Townspeople. And the playing space should be as near level with that community as possible. The play works best in the round or in a three-quarter thrust configuration so that community can be in real *communion* with one another. If your space isn't usually a center for civic engagement, make it so. The object is to lessen the spiritual distance between performer and audience. Eliminating as many of those barriers as possible from the moment we arrive. As such, when the experience nears its end, please consider the idea of bypassing the curtain call. Other than that, there should be as little tech to the design as possible, save flooring that might provide percussive assistance when stomped on.

Audience Participation

This must be subtle and born out of how we connect in real-time. It is how the piece begins and is ingrained in some of the songs' 'call and response' nature. This piece is more conversation than anything. Allow it to be. To that end, VOTE CONDUTION AND MATERIALS are all included at the end of this text.

SONG LIST

[MUSIC NO. 01 – THEN COME BACK AROUND]

[MUSIC NO. 02 – WHAT YA GIVIN' ME?]

[MUSIC NO. 03 – A USED TO BE]

[MUSIC NO. 04 – A USED TO BE (REPRISE)]

[MUSIC NO. 05 – SHOW ME AROUND]

[MUSIC NO. 06 – DO YOU WANNA BE FREE? (PART 1)]

[MUSIC NO. 07 – DO YOU WANNA BE FREE? (PART 2)]

[MUSIC NO. 08 – DO YOU WANNA BE FREE? (PART 3)]

[MUSIC NO. 09 – TEAR THE WHOLE THING DOWN]

[MUSIC NO. 10 – AM I A KING]

[MUSIC NO. 11 – AM I A KING (REPRISE)]

[MUSIC NO. 12 – THEN COME BACK AROUND
    (REPRISE)]

(*The* **MAN** *is seated among the townspeople. The* **MAN** *begins to hum the refrain of*

[MUSIC NO. 01 – THEN COME BACK AROUND].

Offering the melody to the person next to him. Then they offer it to the next person until the hum fills the space and all voices are one. It is both a gentle teaching and a cooperative anchoring. An invitation. Not a requirement. Don't rush it. Allow the townspeople time to find their voice. This moment is an important first step to their understanding that the journey we are about to go on is for and because of them. The **MAN** *might move throughout space – section by section – offering the melody with continued generosity. Once the room is filled with the humming voices of this community, the* **MAN** *suggests the lyrics to the song with the same generosity. Whichever way the townspeople receive this invitation, they are always right. It isn't about the perfection of sound, but that we are choosing to make this sound together. The townspeople are of one voice. This moment takes as long as it needs.*)

MAN.
THEN COME BACK AROUND
THEN COME BACK AROUND
WE ALL COME BACK AROUND
TO THE EDGE OF THIS STREET
THEN COME BACK AROUND

THEN COME BACK AROUND
WE ALL COME BACK AROUND
TO THE EDGE OF THIS STREET
THEN COME BACK AROUND
THEN COME BACK AROUND
WE ALL COME BACK AROUND
TO THE EDGE OF THIS STREET
THEN COME BACK AROUND
THEN COME BACK AROUND
WE ALL COME BACK AROUND
TO THE EDGE OF THIS STREET

And I am grateful! It's no small thing, you know. It's no small thing to say, 'Let these stones behind our backs lay still for a second... before we decide if we gonna use 'em.' It takes a lot to hold off on that. I know... I appreciate it. Seriously. Thank you. Cause I know I done wrong by you but...

The air is still sweet here.

We make it sweet with a collective breath of joy – and suffering too – but mostly *joy*, yeah?

Old men's stories from front porches cast off into the wind blending with
The factory whistle marking the end of the day.
That curious scent children have after recess.
Echoed laughter.
A fried something or a something *baked* from ya mama's kitchen.
Dogs barking and the perfume of changing seasons.
That's *this* air... familiar. Sweet. Air. Familiar.

You thinkin' this air gon' sour.
You thinkin' 'ain't no mo' sweet left to hold!'
But, air made of more than what's been broke.

I ain't sour the air. Don't start that! Please.
And this *is* mine too. It's still mine.

That sweet. I can still have that.

A little bit of that?
Can't I?

Air was sweet the day I came outside of myself and changed your mind on who I was.

It's funny what makes people finally *see you*.
And when they do...

Keep your stones. And hear me out.

    (Beat.)

'Cause on *that* morning, on that same *sweet-aired* morning, there was the hint of something new...

    (To a specific audience member.)

Same mornin' I caught *your* eye seeing me bent over; my back 'bout broke in two.
In a mess a pain. You seen me. You thought I ain't knew.
I could hardly stand. The pain shootin' through me head to toe.
Wished you'd pat me on my shoulder. 'Cause you been there before.
But, you walked on by. 'Cause you had to tend your *own*.

    (To another audience member.)

And you. *You* drove by. Kinda *half*-waved at me.
Guess them children ain't gonna teach themselves.

My road's the one that feeds this town to... 'anywhere but here' and back again.

And I see you all every morning; Sarah, Davey, Doc. Humphrey. Y'all pass me by in a flash of color. A whip of sound. An everydayness that allows the sight of me – bent over and low – play *landmark*. Like our radio station's billboard; chipped paint scattering the grass beneath it. Or, the crooked stop sign no one makes time to fix.

I'm a highway marker saying, 'two miles out from your destination.'

And on *that* morning, I was bent low enough to pick up a piece of earth my mama left me to tend.

But high enough to send

a prayer to the Father.

[MUSIC NO. 02 – WHAT YA GIVIN' ME?]

A HUNDRED SEEDS IN THE SOIL
ONE MORE ROW
AND THE DAY WILL BE WON

WHAT'S A MORNING TO ME?
BUT NEW CALLOUSES ON MY HANDS
AND MORE WORK TO BE DONE

A HUNDRED HOURS IT SEEMS
TOILING OVER BARREN LAND

WHAT'S A SEASON TO ME?
BUT SO LITTLE THAT'S REAPED
FROM THE THINGS I HAD PLANNED

LORD, WHAT I'M ASKIN'
IS TO SEE
        A RETURN

THAT 'TORN DOWN' AND 'WORN OUT'
AIN'T ALL THAT I'VE EARNED
OH, LORD, WHAT I NEED TO KNOW
S'THAT MY EMPTY OLD POCKETS
AIN'T ALL
        THAT I HAVE TO SHOW
        FOR WHAT YA GIVIN' ME
                WHAT YA GIVIN' ME?

And I heard a voice say

STRANGER.
> WOULDN'T YOU LIKE SOME RELIEF?
> WOULDN'T YOU LIKE YOUR DAY TO BREAK EVEN?
> INSTEAD OF BREAKING YOU DOWN...
>
> WOULDN'T YOU LIKE SOME EASE?
> WOULDN'T YOU LIKE SOME RHYME FOR YOUR REASON?
> WOULDN'T YOU LIKE TO HEAR THE SOUND ...
> > OF PROSPERITY?
> > OF PROFIT?
> > OF PEACE?

MAN. Huh? Who's there?

> I'm trying to say a prayer...
> A THOUSAND DAYS HAVE GONE BY
> LIKE A STRANGER
> A VISIT FROM NO ONE
> WHAT'S AN EVENING TO ME?
> SENTIMENTS SHARED WITH MYSELF
> DREAMS BURNT BY THE SUN
> A THOUSAND HOURS IT SEEMS
> PRAYING FOR A LOVIN' TONE
> WHAT'S A HOUSEHOLD TO ME?
> A SIMPLE TOUCH FROM SOMEONE
> WHO COULD MAKE THIS A HOME
> LORD, WHAT I'M ASKIN'
> IS TO SEE
> > A RETURN
> THAT 'TORN DOWN' AND 'WORN OUT'
> AIN'T ALL THAT I EARNED
> OH, LORD, WHAT I NEED TO KNOW
> S'THAT MY EMPTY OLD HEART
> AIN'T ALL
> > THAT I HAVE TO SHOW
> > FOR WHAT YA GIVIN' ME
> > WHAT YA GIVIN' ME?

> And I heard a voice say

STRANGER.
>WOULDN'T YOU LIKE SOME RELIEF?
>WOULDN'T YOU LIKE YOUR DAY TO BREAK EVEN?
>INSTEAD OF BREAKING YOU DOWN...
>
>WOULDN'T YOU LIKE SOME EASE?
>WOULDN'T YOU LIKE SOME RHYME FOR YOUR REASON?
>WOULDN'T YOU LIKE TO HEAR THE SOUND ...
>>OF PROSPERITY?
>>OF PROFIT?
>>OF PASSION   AND PEACE?

Because that's how I come...

In Peace, brother.

MAN. *(Catching his breath.)* And I looked him up and down.
I looked him up and right back down.
He look *familiar*...
Like from some kinda unwanted yesterday and some kinda fear for tomorrow.
But, that fear gave way to something easy in him...

STRANGER. Say you ain't been seen?
Well, now...
That there?
Yeah, that ain't exactly true.

MAN. His skin could have been his suit!
Or, the other way around.

He was golden wheat.
And gold itself.

STRANGER. You're staring.

MAN. I ask who his people was.
His mama 'nem.
I ask 'bout his work. His line.
Hey, what you do, old man?

STRANGER. To pass the time?

MAN. For a living?

STRANGER. One in the same.
I grant the downtrodden some wishes.
Some *salve* for their pain.

Oh, I been watching you. You ain't been alone. Your sad little song had an audience.

You ain't been singing to no moon.
While *you* harvest these fields
I harvest sad tunes.

Someone's always listening.

MAN. Someone? Who?

STRANGER. Oh, just the someone... meant for you.

When I whispered your name
Only you could hear it.
See, my brother, I'm just the hallelujah for your spirit.

MAN. His hallelujah ain't come with no stompin' foot.
Ain't come with no shout.
Just that tiny *whisper* he was talking about.

Just enough to knead at the knot of my *loneliness*. A welcome sight in a home with one chair.

You want coffee? Cup of tea?

STRANGER. Oh. For little ole me?
Sure. Sure.
Don't mind if I do.
But while we sip
I just want to sit there
And talk about you.

MAN. Me?

STRANGER. Yes. You. Is that something new?

MAN. Most folks don't ask.

STRANGER. Not even a simple, 'How do you do?'
    What a shame.
    What. A. Shame.

MAN. Then, he looked *me* up and down. And down and
    right back up.

STRANGER. Oh. A grimace to boot?

MAN. *(Holds his back.)* Yeah. 'bout twenty years stooped.

STRANGER. Oh. What a shame.
    What. A. Shame.

    Shall we?

MAN. Headin' up toward the house, his walk was
    something silk woven.
    Navigating each turn with ease.
    While mine was burlap'd with ache and time.
    He opened my door like he had the keys!

STRANGER. Now, if you don't mind…

MAN. He pulled two cups out of the cupboard and onto
    the table.
    We sat there for a minute. Just being easy.
    He placed his jacket on the back of the chair
    Then melded himself there
    Into the house like a piece of old furniture.
    Certain. Steady. Breezy.

STRANGER. I'll take that tea please.

MAN. A moment. Breath. Grin.
    And then…

STRANGER. Now, tell me what might have a man like you
    stressed?

MAN. Uh.

STRANGER. Meaning, the source of your unhappiness.

What might a man like you need?

MAN. Friends! Money?

STRANGER. Hush! I ain't talkin' about greed.

Superficial things.
Things won't make you happy.

Friends are *fickle*.
Think bigger!

MAN. Bigger?

STRANGER. Huh. De*spicable*.

You don't even know, do you?

MAN. Know what?

A moment. Breath. Grin.
And then...

From out his pocket came the sweetest of liquor.

STRANGER. You feel free to have a sip or
Hey, brother, have your fill.
Go on close your eyes now.
And hold still.

MAN. My mind floating. Body warm to the touch.
Riding a wave of this newfound *company*.
And I'm thinking about a village of turned *backs*.
Of car after *truck* after neighbor just like *that* – passing
me by
His voice was
a comfort to me.

[MUSIC 03 – A USED TO BE]

STRANGER. Now, brother, let me tell you a little bit about
what I *see*.

(In tempo.) Starting with these old road signs.
That little piece of highway?
That battered up downtown.

Or, should I say
'A USED TO BE.'

That's where we are.

In 'A USED TO BE.'

(In tempo.) Take a tired old suit. Right?

Hanging in your closet.
Add the number of times
You   stopped and started

'Round
Meeting someone lovely,
Putting it on,
Hitting the town.
But, now...
That suit's
'A USED TO BE.'
(You can't fit it anymore)
It's A 'USED TO BE.'
SEE, A 'USED TO BE'
IS A 'ONCE WAS'
AND A
'ONCE WAS' IS 'A DREAM'
AND WHEN IT'S GOES
IT SHOWS.
IT LEAVES A SHADOW
A SHELL
A REGRET
MIGHT AS WELL TAKE THIS
REMINDER OF ...
WHAT 'USED TO BE.'
(Get my drift)
A 'USED TO BE.'

(In tempo.) And that crick in your back
Where there   once was freedom.
And this dried dust's fruit
When you couldn't wait to eat 'em!

Where there was a *there*... there?
A 'USED TO BE ...'

MAN. Oh, I see what
You're sayin.
I USED TO BE.
THIS USED TO BE

STRANGER.
BUT IT DON'T HAVE TO BE.

MAN.
IT DON'T HAVE TO BE ...

STRANGER. Watch me.

MAN. A moment. Breath. Grin.
And then...

He cracked a toothy smile that, I swear,

Filled whatever grooves heavy shadows had etched
themselves there

Into the floorboards.

A smile that silenced whistling from an aging roof.
Pictures faded on beveled walls suddenly restored,
Lord!

My home was at once a worthy space to fill.

STRANGER. Now, let me set your wavering *foundation*
still.
A hallelujah for your spirit, brother!
Or, What you will.

MAN.
LOOK WHAT YOU GIVEN' ME.
LOOK WHAT YOU GIVEN' ME!

We talked of loves lost and others gained.
Trading stories from my youth like he had been a
witness!
For every heartache recalled,
A hand-covered shoulder.
For every *remembrance* of darkness
A *knowing glance* and a focus in.

A 'hm.'
A 'yes!'
And a   'sho you right!'
You see, by the end of the night...
I had a friend.

A little more liquor and a round of tall tales
Sent a howling laughter – a wail –
Pure from *his* gut aimed square at *my* chest,
Breaking it open!

My arms wide spread exhaling a long-abandoned crest
Of *joy* OHHHH!!
Inhaling the promise of a new day!

(Looks out. A delighted surprise.)

Ha. Mornin'?

STRANGER. Mornin'?

Oh, I should get goin'!

MAN. Goin'?

STRANGER. Goin'.
It's almost mornin'.
Yeah, I don't do so well in the brightness of light.
I do most of my operating in the gentle dark of night.
And, I'm sure you have more work to do.
Have to get on with your day.
So, thank you for the chitter chatter.
But, I really shouldn't overstay
My welcome.

MAN. But, you ain't gonna let me pay you back?

STRANGER. Oh. You're welcome.

MAN. No! I mean, you're in such a hurry.
Do you really have to go?

What you goin' home *to?*
You got people?

STRANGER. Well... no.

To be honest, brother,
I'm kinda like you.
And I've been curious 'bout what a little change of
scenery could do for me too.

MAN. Then let *me* help *you!*

And I looked down at my hands empty as ever.
The house *I'm* standing in beautified by *his* touch.

Didn't you enjoy the time we had together? Didn't you
at least enjoy that much?

I'll be ya people! Friendship's what I got.
I ain't got much else to give.

STRANGER. Says who?
These same ungrateful people
Here where you live?

[MUSIC NO. 04 – A USED TO BE (REPRISE)]

You know, I answer many a callin' but, yours was the
first open door.
Your heart is so big. I couldn't ask it to do more.

But...

(Considers.)

A manifestation
Of equal compensation
Divided by the potential in you.

And oh! It's so clear,
Sweet brother my dear,
The greater sum of the 'what' you could do!

MAN. Huh?

STRANGER. You see how I
Just took your 'used to be'
Sifted it through a 'might have been'

Sprinkled on a 'coulda'
'Shoulda'
'Woulda'

And got...
A 'STILL COULD BE?'

Like this house.

MAN. Oh.
A 'STILL COULD BE ...'

STRANGER. And what's more
'A better than!'

Because a friend to you right now
Is a waving hand.
And you'd be happy with just a touch of green
Popping out of this land.

But, what this *town really* needs
Is a someone like *you*
To take them beyond the glory of *their* 'used to'
Into
A 'better than.'

MAN. Me?

STRANGER. Oh, yes, my man.

MAN. So... me changing this town for the better
How's that do you any good?

STRANGER. Oh, my brother,

Yours ain't the only spirit
That's been wildly misunderstood.

[MUSIC NO. 05 – SHOW ME AROUND]

SEE, JUST TO INFORM YOU, THE FORM YOU SEE BEFORE
    YOU RIGHT NOW
IS NEVER MUCH OF *TOO* MUCH FOR *TOO* LONG
AS A MATTER OF FACT, I'M A FORM QUITE MATTERLESS
AND BY DAWN A BODY LIKE MY BODY IS GONE.

SO, NOW YOU KNOW ME
BUT, I'D LIKE TO KNOW THIS *TOWN*
I THINK *YOU* KNOW *THEM*
WANT YOU TO SHOW ME AROUND

'CAUSE I'VE TRIED TO EMBODY THE BODIES OF REGULAR
    ANYBODIES
THE KIND OF HUMANS KINDLY TO HUMANKIND
BUT, THE MORE I PRESS INTO A BODY, I'M LESS
    IMPRESSED MORE OR LESS
YOUR GOOEY INNARDS SURE DON'T ENDURE OVER TIME

I COULDN'T FEEL IT YOU SEE
BUT, I'D LIKE TO FEEL THIS *TOWN*
I THINK *YOU* FEEL *THEM*
WANT YOU TO SHOW ME AROUND

'CAUSE THERE'S A CHANCE, PERCHANCE TO CHANGE MY
    DRIFTER'S CIRCUMSTANCE
RESOURCING ANOTHER SOURCE, OF COURSE, FOR A SOUL
WITH A TOWN, IF YOU GET MY INF'RENCE, A SOUL IS
    QUITE DIFF'RENT
IT'S PERMENANT EVEN WHEN ITS TENANTS TEND TO
    COME AND GO

SEE, GRIND CITY'S GOT BEALE
EMERALD CITY IT'S NEEDLE
AND THE BIG APPLE'S THE CITY THAT NEVER SLEEPS
THIS TOWN'S GOT A SOUL THAT I KINDA DIG

AND I'M ON A MISSION TO CEMENT MY OWN LEGACY

BUT, I'M A LOST ONE

THE SAME AS YOU IN THIS TOWN

BUT WE COULD FIND AN *US* HERE

IF YOU SPREAD A LITTLE ME AROUND

COME ON NOW, HELP ME BUILD IT

AND MAKE YOUR OWN MARK ON THIS TOWN

CAUSE IF I KNOW YOU

I THINK YOU LIKE THE WAY THAT SOUNDS

MAN. Oh, I don't know 'bout all that...

Friendship's plenty for me.

STRANGER. Brother, what you'd get in exchange for impressing my name and *only* my name upon this town is something more valuable than any trinket or fair-weather!

Fools are befriended on purpose, Man.

Come on now, you know better!

MAN. So are kings...

STRANGER. Ahhh. Huh. Okay. Clever.

Kings and fools are befriended on purpose.
None of them purposes ever good.
But, *sagacious* men of true esteem
Are *revered* in return.
Now, is that a place *you've* ever stood?

MAN. Shoot, I'm barely standing as it is.

STRANGER. *Admiration* makes for longevity.
Keeps people by your side.
A deeper thing than any ole half-hearted handwave could provide.

A Solid alliance: Me and you.

Deliver to your neighbors this *joy* I'm offering. And that's what you can expect.

Enduring legacy. Respect!

MAN. Respect?

STRANGER. Oh heck.

I seem to have struck a nerve.

Let me offer you a plan to get what you truly deserve.

MAN. Then, in my right hand, he placed Seeds and a golden Spade,

STRANGER. Just a little break of the earth in the corner of a lot. One Seed. A whole field of lusciousness grows out of nothing.

MAN. In my left hand a golden Scythe

STRANGER. Cutting down the old so that new can grow.

MAN. Then he said

STRANGER. And know. And know.

The Seed, The Scythe and the Spade don't just work on land.

That is the power to change *a people* resting in your hand!

But, these gadgets are of *me*. Remember that.

And changing this town in my image is at the root of this pact.

MAN. And if that pact don't hold somehow?

STRANGER. Well, now...

Of course, the image of me comes with... a slight risk.

What the *town* is gonna see is a *fabrication* of their every wish.

Wishes live in a hopeful dream space!

And the *gleam* in their eyes, will *shape* what's in front of their face.

That's the *joy* you will be giving.

MAN. But how is that really living?
We'll be holding on to nothing.

STRANGER. Oh, my friend, dreams *are* something!
And, here's the thing, I'm making *your* dreams come
true.
What I do for *you* will always be the real deal.
What I give to *them* will have, let's say, an outstanding
outward appeal!

But, if the pact somehow *does* get broken,
Every dream in this town will become awoken
Back to reality.
Even yours.
And a *darker* one at that.
My best advice? Is uh... don't break the pact.

Hey! Take that spade and try scratching your back!

MAN. And I reached over my shoulder and let the tip of
that spade
Hit me right between my shoulder blades.

STRANGER. Down. Down. Down
Yeah, just like that!

MAN. And a Crack. Crack. Crack. What's that...?

(*His spine straightens. He suddenly limber.*)

Ohhhhh...
Free...
Free...
I ...
Feel like the old me.
No... I felt like a *new* me!!

STRANGER. You like that kinda free?
You feel that possibility?

What *joyful* gifts you could bring!
Now, go out there

Look your kinfolk in the eye, brother,
Sing!

[MUSIC NO. 06 – DO YOU WANNA BE FREE? (PART 1)]

MAN.

I KNOW I WANNA BE FREE
DO YOU WANNA BE FREE?

HEY. I SAY.
DO YOU WANNA BE FREE?
DO YOU WANNA BE FREE?

Ohhhhh, Yessir! If that's the kinda fixin' up that you say I can give.
That's *exactly* the kinda *joy* that I wanna spread. Yessir!

STRANGER. Good! Good!
Tell them, good man!

MAN.

I KNOW I WANNA BE
FREE
DO YOU WANNA BE
FREE?

HEY. I SAY.
DO YOU WANNA BE FREE?
DO YOU WANNA BE FREE?

I GOT A BEND NOW IN MY BACK
I GOT A SONG NOW HOW 'BOUT THAT
I GOT A SEED TO GROW
A RIGHTEOUS LOVE

I GOT A HEP NOW IN MY STEP
I GOT A MOVE NOW IN MY GROOVE
I GOT THE ANSWER TO THE *WHAT*
YOU BEEN THINKING OF

I KNOW I WANNA BE

FREE

DO YOU WANNA BE

FREE?

HEY. I SAY.

DO YOU WANNA BE FREE?

DO YOU WANNA BE FREE?

STRANGER. Ah, Good!

(Suddenly serious.) Now look here. Go on spread that love,

Or whatever you think this is a feeling of,

To the many.

There's plenty

To go around.

Ladle it out for those smack-lipped paupers hungry for a change.

Hungry for their worlds to rearrange.

But, let them know the *how's* and the *why's* and *whose* of it all.

Let them know it's *me* who's Major of this bacchanal.

My name should be written wherever you stop

Or set up shop

To heal the aching hearted.

Remember this town's soul is mine... the moment you get started.

MAN. And with that he departed.

A moment. Breath.

(He grins.) Henh.

[MUSIC NO. 07 – DO YOU WANNA BE FREE? (PART 2)]

(Slow build.)

I KNOW I WANNA BE FREE

DO YOU WANNA BE

FREE?

HEY. I SAY.

DO YOU WANNA BE FREE?
DO YOU WANNA BE FREE?

(In tempo.)

I GOT A BEND NOW IN MY BACK
I GOT A SONG NOW HOW 'BOUT THAT
I GOT A SEED TO GROW
A RIGHTEOUS LOVE

Yes! And I took that Scythe. Like to have one hand 'round ya partner. Small of her back tucked deep in the crux of your elbow. I let my hip sink. Bent that knee a little. Wound her back. And took a few smooth swings like to lead a waist slow dragging on a Saturday night.

Swoosh. Swoosh. Swoosh! Hey!

And all that was overgrown and weed-choked turn into the richest of mulch wet-soil. I stabbed that Spade down in the corner of my newly cleared acre, just how he told me to do. Picked a simple Seed from the bunch he give me. Dropped it right into the sweet dirt. Stood back and...

Ohhh, children!

I GOT THE ANSWER   TO THE *WHAT*
YOU BEEN DREAMING OF
I KNOW I WANNA BE
FREE
DO YOU WANNA BE
FREE?
HEY. I SAY.
DO YOU WANNA BE FREE?
DO YOU WANNA BE FREE?

All them kids from *your* class came runnin' out to see the commotion. Neighbors stickin' they heads out of windows. Cars slowed to a halt to see them tomato vines curling spirals up into the air like mudras

summoned from a dancer's wrist. Melons so ripe their
sugar make your nostrils open like a whop't man to his
forever lover!

HEY. I SAY.

DO YOU WANNA BE FREE

DO YOU WANNA BE FREE

OH, I CAN SEE YOU PRESSING BY

BUT, COME ON AND LOOK ME IN THE EYE

ONCE YOU DO

YOU'LL NEVER BE THE SAME

Then here come all y'all. Gathering round me.

Here come a Sarah say, 'Hey now you look like you
standing 'bout ten feet tall!'

Here come a Davey say, 'Look at your field and the
fruit it yield. That house of yours! Tight!' Here come a
Bobby say, 'Hey now, you hit that number? You wished
on a star? Got yourself a rabbit's foot?'

Here come a Doc. Humphry say, 'Naw. That's elbow
grease right there. Persistence. Prayer.'

Here come a everybody say, 'I need a little bit' a what
you got!'

Here come a, 'Hey now... what's your secret?'

SAID, I CAN SEE YOU PRESSING BY

BUT, COME ON LOOK ME IN THE EYE

ONCE YOU DO

YOU'LL NEVER BE THE SAME

IF LIFE'S GOT YOU FEELING LOW

JUST WAIT AND REAP HERE WHAT I SOW

I USE THESE TOOLS

TO MAKE LIGHT OF YOUR PAIN

> *(Guides audience to 'Yeah. Yeah.' A call and
> response.)*

DO YOU WANNA BE

FREE?

MAN & AUDIENCE.

YEAH. YEAH

MAN.

IF YOU WANNA BE FREE

SAY YEAH

HEY. I SAY.

DO YOU WANNA BE FREE?

DO YOU WANNA BE FREE?

MAN & AUDIENCE.

YEAH. YEAH

MAN.

DO YOU WANNA BE FREE?

MAN & AUDIENCE.

YEAH. YEAH

MAN.

DO YOU WANNA BE FREE?

MAN & AUDIENCE.

YEAH. YEAH

MAN.

HEY. I SAY.

DO YOU WANNA BE FREE?

DO YOU WANNA BE FREE?

And here I come... to suddenly having y'all visit. *Everyone* in this town. Every snaggle-toothed. Every wide-eyes. Every sure stance. Every *he* nosey. And can't keep *her* mouth shut. Every humming when he cooks. Every staring at the engine with the hood of the car popped up sipping a beer and nodding into nothingness. Every hand on her hip about to fuss. Everyone of y'all... Looking at me for a thing *I* had to offer. And here I come to a' understanding that my road ain't no longer just a mile marker. Ain't a 'get through.'

It's a 'stay a while.' It's a 'get to know me.' *(Pure Joy.)* **A** get to know... *me*?

Here come a pat on the back.
Here come a flower in my hair.
Here come a hand shake.
Here come a, 'Say, uh... what else you think you can fix up like that with them tools there? You ain't gon' keep that good all to yourself, is you?'

A moment. A breath... *(Slow claps. Call and response.)*

[MUSIC NO. 08 – DO YOU WANNA BE FREE? (PART 3)]

LOOK LIKE YOU WANNA BE FREE

MAN & AUDIENCE.

YEAH. YEAH

MAN.

DO YOU WANNA BE FREE?

MAN & AUDIENCE.

YEAH. YEAH

MAN.

HEY. I SAY.
DO YOU WANNA BE FREE
DO YOU WANNA BE FREE

MAN & AUDIENCE.

YEAH. YEAH

MAN.

YOU HIT YOURSELF AN UNLUCKY STREAK
AIN'T GOT NO FOOD IN YOUR HOUSE TO EAT
YOU STARVING FOR
WHAT YOU THOUGHT WAS IMPOSSIBLE

YOU WANT THIS PLACE HERE FIXED UP NICE?
YOU GONNA WANNA TAKE SOME OF MY ADVICE

I GOT THE ANSWER TO THE *WHAT*
YOU BEEN DREAMING OF

I CAN HELP YOU GET FREE

MAN & AUDIENCE.
YEAH. YEAH

MAN.
I CAN HELP YOU GET FREE

MAN & AUDIENCE.
YEAH. YEAH

MAN.
HEY. I SAY
I CAN HELP YOU GET FREE
I CAN HELP YOU GET FREE

MAN & AUDIENCE.
YEAH. YEAH

MAN.
I CAN HELP YOU GET FREE

MAN & AUDIENCE.
YEAH. YEAH

MAN.
I CAN HELP YOU GET FREE

MAN & AUDIENCE.
YEAH. YEAH

MAN.
HEY. I SAY
I CAN HELP YOU GET FREE
I CAN HELP YOU GET FREE

MAN & AUDIENCE.
YEAH. YEAH

MAN. Here come a, 'Well, why don't you stop all that damn singing and tell us somethin', man!'

And that was the *first* time we came together like we are right now.

When I could see every waiting eye that's had a blindin' trouble here and there.

Your hearts' beating set a pace for the wanting of a life more fair.

And here I stood with the remedy.

'Now, look here,' I say.
'Remember on this day

The story I say...
Of a man in a suit of gold.'

And the children's bodies leaned forward. Men and women as old as the dust grew younger in their hope with each word that left my mouth.

And here come a, 'Hey, now what kind of liquor you say he gave you! You still high as kite ain't you! You fooling us or what?'
Here come a, 'Let the man speak! Keep going, now.'

Then, I held out the gifts he give me; The Seed, The Scythe and The Spade.
And did a little demonstration on how a wonder gets made.
Backed up a little just outside my own yard.
Cleared that old, planted that Seed.
Then, here come a, 'Oh. My. God. See there! That man wasn't lying! He got magic in him now!'

And here come Doc. Humphrey say, 'Yeah, but tell me how?
This fella in his golden suit don't sound like your typical fare.
And I have heard of stories like this before and I'm thinking buyer beware.

What it cost? What it cost to have your place this pristine?'

'Don't look like it cost him nothing, Doc!
He standing up straight. He looking clean!'
    A voice... way in the back.

Here come a, 'Well, did he have horns on his head?
And little tail with an arrowed point on the end?
Did his face turn up in a Cheshire grin?'

    (Hesitation.)

That suit of gold was all *I* saw him fitted in.

'Hm,' Doc. say, 'Hm. So, we can have *all* of this fortune?
Just the *same* as you?
Everything *you* got *we* can get for next to nothin'?
And there's no doubtin' in your mind that's true?'

    (More hesitation.)

All that matters... is what a thing called *joy* looks like to you.

    (A decision.)

Remember on this day the story I say of a man who wanted to... *shape a town.*

I could paint a pretty picture with my words but come on, y'all. Look around.
Now, only those who truly desire the help I can provide will get it.
Ain't no pressure for those who don't wish to change.
No pressure if you're contented.
It's all on *you*, what you'd have me do.

And here come a, 'Man shiiii –'

[MUSIC NO. 09 – TEAR THE WHOLE THING DOWN]

TOWNSPERSON.

TEAR THE WHOLE THING *DOWN*

MAN.

WHAT?

TOWNSPERSON.

YEAH. TEAR THE DAMN THING DOWN

OKAY.

AYES AND NAYS

AND NO HALF WAYS

LET'S VOTE

I SAY

TEAR IT ALL DOWN.

TOWNSPERSON (WOMAN).

TESTIMONIAL!

NOW, *I* BEEN TEACHING AT THE *COUNTY* HIGH SCHOOL

FOR *20* SOME ODD YEARS OR *SO*

BOOKS ABOUT AS OLD AS I AM

NO SUP*PLIES*. CRACKED WALLS AND *FLOORS*

NOW, *RAISE* YOUR HAND JUST LIKE MY STUDENTS

IF YOU *THINK* WE COULD LEARN A LESSON

'BOUT *CAPITALIZING* ON AN *IN*VESTMENT

AND NOT DE*NYING* OURSELVES A BLESSING

TEAR THE WHOLE THING DOWN

MAN.

WHAT?

TOWNSPERSON (WOMAN).

YEAH. TEAR THE DAMN THING DOWN

OKAY.

AYES AND NAYS

AND NO HALF WAYS

LET'S VOTE

I SAY

TEAR IT ALL DOWN.

TOWNSPERSON (MAN).

TESTIMONIAL!

NOW, *I* BELIEVE IN A*BUN*DANCE
AS PART OF MY SPIRITUALITY.
I BELIEVE THERE IS MORE IN *STORE* FOR YOU
(AND IF IT SELLS THE *FINER* THINGS THEN
THAT *STORE'S* FOR ME)

BUT, RAISE YOUR HAND IF YOU EVER FEEL
LIKE *CERTAIN* STORES STAY *SHUT*
AND ALL THAT YOU AC*CUM*ULATE
IS DE*VALUED* NO MATTER WHAT!
TEAR THE WHOLE THING DOWN

MAN.

WHAT?

TOWNSPERSON (MAN).

YEAH. TEAR THE DAMN THING DOWN
OKAY.

AYES AND NAYS
AND NO HALF WAYS
LET'S VOTE
I SAY
　　　TEAR IT ALL DOWN.

TOWNSPERSON (MIDDLE-AGED MAN).

TESTIMONIAL!

SAY THAT YOU HAVE BEEN A RESIDENT HERE
FOR ALL YOUR NATURAL *LIFE*
YOU *RAISE* A FAMILY, HAVE SOME KIDS
WITH YOUR　BEAUTIFUL WIFE.

THEN ONE DAY THEM *KIDS*
FIND THEMSELVES GETTING OLDER
RAISE YOUR HAND IF YOUR NEST IS EMPTY
CAUSE THERE'S NO *JOBS* LEFT HERE TO HOLD 'EM.
TEAR THE WHOLE THING *DOWN*

MAN.
> WHAT?

TOWNSPERSON (MIDDLE-AGED MAN).
> YEAH. TEAR THE DAMN THING DOWN
> OKAY.
>
> AYES AND NAYS
> AND NO HALF WAYS
> LET'S VOTE
> I SAY
>> TEAR IT ALL DOWN.

TOWNSPERSON (OLD WOMAN).
> TESTIMONIAL!
>
> NOW, WAIT WAIT WAIT WAIT
> WAIT WAIT WAIT WAIT WAIT
>
> I DISSENT. MY BRETHREN, I DISSENT.
> NOW, I HEAR AND FEEL ALL Y'ALLS ARGUMENTS
> BUT, I SWEAR TO GOD THERE'S A *HERE* ALREADY *HERE*
>
> NOW, *RAISE* YOUR HAND IF YOU *THINK*
> WE *HAVE* AN IDENTITY
> AND *WE* JUST CAN'T GO OFF
> SO EASILY *SELLING* OUR HISTORY

MAN. A moment. A Breath.

TOWNSPERSON (OLD WOMAN).
> TEAR THE WHOLE THING DOWN

MAN.
> WHAT?

TOWNSPERSON (OLD WOMAN).
> YEAH. TEAR THE DAMN THING DOWN
> OKAY.
>
> AYES AND NAYS
> AND NO HALF WAYS
> LET'S VOTE
> I SAY
>> TEAR IT ALL DOWN.

TOWNSPERSON (DOC. HUMPHREY).

TESTIMONIAL!

NOW, *BOTTOM* LINE IS THIS BROTHER HERE

SAY WE GOT *ONE* OF TWO WAYS TO GO

PUT THE GOLDEN FELLAH'S NAME

ON A HANDFUL OF SIGNS

IT'S A *SIMPLE* YES OR NO

OR, WE COULD JUST KEEP ON LIVING LIFE

WITH NO FURTHER INCIDENT

BUT, *RAISE* YOUR HAND IF SOMEBODY ELSE

SQUASHING OUR CHANCE

IS A THING YOU MIGHT *RESENT*

TEAR THE WHOLE THING DOWN

MAN.

FINE

TOWNSPERSON (DOC. HUMPHREY).

YEAH. TEAR THE DAMN THING DOWN

OKAY.

AYES AND NAYS

NO HALF WAYS

LET'S VOTE

(Call and response. **DOC. HUMPHREY** *calls 'What?' Audience builds to 'Tear the whole thing down.')*

TEAR THE WHOLE THING DOWN.

WHAT?

TEAR THE WHOLE THING DOWN

WHAT?

TEAR THE WHOLE THING DOWN

WHAT?

TEAR THE WHOLE THING DOWN

WHAT?

MAN. We *voted*...
To tear the whole thing down.

(A moment.)

I told you the story of the man in gold?
I said to you... all he said to me?

(A moment.)

I took up in my hands The Seed, The Scythe, and The Spade.
The weight of each much heavier by the decision that we made.

Together.

And here come a, 'Well, what's all the waiting for? We done voted ain't we? Come on now, brother. Lead the way!'

And we took off to walk about town marking things 'leanin',
'Unnecessary,' 'broke beyond repair,'
Or... 'a memory.'
We labeled things 'forget.'
Touched on some 'queen of diamonds in a bicycle spoke' memory.
Pushed through a wedding day in the one room church.
Say baptism.
And too many funerals.
Say going home, going home, home going.
Marked things a 'used to be.' A 'once upon a time.'
Say waiting in line to send packages
And notes from far away.
Fingers run across each tear-drop stained letter
Say she's never seen the likes of these bloodied battlefields
But, she aching for a home cooked meal.
We spotted trees

Say etched into

Like to promise a heart with initials added together at its center.

A sum of sweet sweet hopes and histories sweet.

And we marched on

Clearing spaces once made of jagged holes dug so far down into

That there are whispers of children bragging 'bout making it to the other side of the world

Echoing from within 'em.

Gentle laughter teasing.

And the old folks

Fussing...

We reached the corner of town. Right where 'somewhere else' and 'exactly where you are' tend to cross.

And here come a, 'What you waiting on? Do that thang with the spade, man!'

And swoosh. And break of soil. And planted seed.

And here come a 'Here's to a new life!'

And an 'Amen'

Amen

Amen

And

[MUSIC NO. 10 – AM I A KING]

BORROWED PAINTED PICTURE LIKE

BORROWED PAINTED PICTURE VIEWS OF

BORROWED PAINTED PICTURE VIEWS OF SOMETHING
   RARE HERE

RARE HERE

COUNTRY ROAD SOFT

     LIKE   COUNTRY ROAD SOFT FOCUSED

COUNTRY ROAD SOFT FOCUSED BUT IN A DIFFERENT HUE

HERE
WHAT COULD WE DO HERE?

With my spade sunk in the earth. Like those fruits. Like all the magic, and like all the memories that came before it. The soft roll of change starts to take shape.

WHAT COULD WE DO HERE?

AUTHOR WRITES A STORY
AN AUTHOR WRITES A STORY ON A CROWDED
PAGE
AUTHOR KEEPS A HISTORY
WRITES A PLAY
FOR A NEW STAGE

And one by one each *building* rises taller and taller. Each *road* gets paved in wonder. Each *field* sees a bounty like to last us forever. The plenty for the few.

'CAUSE GOLD IS ALL THE RAGE
YES, GOLD IS ALL THE RAGE NOW
GOLD IS ALL THE RAGE
NOW

And I suddenly feel air under my feet. Then a sinking in my stomach as if in flight. And I am *lifted* up on shoulders!

KEYS TO THE TOWN
KEYS TO THE TOWN NOW
I CAN WEAR A CROWN NOW
YES, I CAN WEAR A CROWN
NOW
TILTED TO THE SIDE.

AM I A KING
AM I A KING
OR JUST A FOOL

Eyes widen as we walk the streets of this shiny unfamiliar. And Ohhs and so many Ahhs.

What's that moment when your spirit finally sees what your children see in you? Hero. Protector. Smartest person in the room. And that wealth of responsibility and expectation washes over you... in fear. I never knew I could be as big as y'all imagined me to be. We walked the length of this town like to have all y'alls hope pressed into *my* chest. A hope we didn't think possible.

A still could be?
A better than?
  WE DIDN'T KNOW

And like those new gleaming buildings, that change came gunning for us too.
Here come a, 'Man, we looking fit today, y'all!'
As we turned to see suited up, dressed to the nines and church hats beaming. Seersucker, loafer, high heeled and high steppin' all. All shades of royal set into our gaits.
Here come a, 'Man! I could get used to this!'
  CAUSE' GOLD IS ALL THE RAGE
        YES, GOLD IS ALL THE RAGE NOW
  GOLD IS ALL THE RAGE
        NOW
  AM I A KING
        AM I?

We all skip hop skip down the street. Like how we *guess* easy moments to be. Borrowed images of hope from some film we seen as kids maybe? Smiles curled. Sight sharpened.
Here come a, 'When I step foot in my new house...'
Here come a, 'Can't nobody tell me nothin!'
Here come a, 'You ain't ate no pies like the pies I'm 'bout to bake from the fruit in my orchard, baby!'
Here come, 'Just watch me stunning in that new car. Crusin' like what!'

Here come a, 'Imma be the person I wished I could be with this new money way of living.'

AM I A KING

AM I A KING

Our imaginations set us into motion. The months pass. And gold becomes a throw away thing like water, air or that morning kiss goodbye. We don't even notice the unusual unusualness of it. Easy from a faucet easy.

THE DAYS MIGHT STILL PASS BY

        THE DAYS THEY DO GO BY

TIP OF THE HAT

        HELLO GOODNIGHT

THEY STILL PASS BY

        THE DAYS ...

BUT THIS TIME THERE'S A GLANCE

        A SMILING LITTLE GLANCE (FOR ME)

IT'S ALL WORTH IT.

And every day there's *you*. Come to *me*. Asking me for a little blessing here and there. Lay a hand on a new baby's head.

Here come *me* saying, 'Well, now, you wanna see if Cooper's got that steed ready for breeding come May.'

Here come me saying, 'Ain't nothing the two of you can't work out. Love will find a way.'

Here come me saying, 'Sell 'em for about five cents cheaper. Seem fair enough. She's you neighbor. Keep her.'

Admiration. Respect.

WAS IT WORTH IT?

Real friendship...

AM I A KING

AM I A KING

How high? How high? How high can a man be?
Life saver y'all say. Statue center of town. Of ME.

AM I A KING

Townsquare. Pageantry! Music! And favorite color painted faces. And all on *this* day to celebrate our storied walk into this... *newness*. Feasts of fruits without a blemish.

And as the wine flows
My speech goes...

A town ain't nothing but history waiting for future!
And we turned our future to good that day.

Here come a, 'Yes. Yes.
You bettah preach, now.
You bettah go on! What you say!'

Towns are built by its people. That's you. And that's the person to ya side.

Here come a 'Yes. Yes!'

I'm talking 'bout a kind of *joyful* building. One that lessens the divide
Between us.
'Cause between *us*...
That joyful *building*
Is us building joyfulness from the *inside*.

And that edifice? It don't just stand on joy.
It stands on our duty to one another.
An edifice built on how we call each other sister
And how we call each other brother.
Here come a,

TOWNSPERSON ('LITTLE HORNS' LADY). 'Yes! Yes! Yes! Yes! Now, wait a minute!
If a town is built by an 'us'; how you say, 'the people to ya side?'
Then, who is this 'he' that claims it?
This 'he' who made us re-name it.
Seems like his portion is a bit... outsized.'

MAN. Here come a

TOWNSPERSON (DAVEY). 'Yeah, he ain't been here not a once.

I mean, we ain't never *seen't* 'im.

His name *stay* fixed on a place *we* built.

A place *we* built. If I get your meanin'.

Say, wasn't *you* the first one to set that spade into land?'

MAN. Sure... sure. I was. And... I understand. But, –

TOWNSPERSON (ORCHARD LADY). 'And *I'm* the one work *my* land every day.

These hands. These hands.

A concrete thing.

Folks run they own shops

Live on streets they've had for years...

Look like we put the '*joyful* work' in, but the town's still... his?"

MAN. But, he's been a real friend to this town. And to me.

TOWNSPERSON (OLD WOMAN). 'How can you stay friends with a friend you never see...?

Seem like 'the people to ya side' take friendship just a hair more seriously

Friendship look like community. Those folks who stays around.

Look like us folks who moved you from the *edge* to the *center* of this town.'

MAN. *(Smiles.)* Yes, right at its center...

My dearest friends. Believe me, I remember.

TOWNSPERSON (OLD WOMAN). 'Solid chasing vapor don't seem legit.

Now, how 'bout we put *your* name on this town?

How you feel that sit?'

(Points to several audience members.)

Here come a 'Yes. Yes. Yes. Yes. Yes. Yes. Yes. Yes. Yes.
Yes'

A moment. A breath.
And then
A grin
And grin
And grin
And...

I think... that's the *perfect* name for it!

What was in the heart of that pied piper
guiding children to their end?
If you recall the story in the beginning,
When that town was so desperate to rid itself of plague,
    They also called him a friend.

STRANGER. Well! Don't you all look nice?
   I mean, the physical town, to be more precise

No one invited me to this little renaming party
No one asked for my input at all.
Did you not think I might have something to say about
it?
I mean, come on y'all. Come on, y'all!

And, then there's my brother here. His heart leaping
out of his chest.
Out of all of you, it's him I'm most disappointed in.
But, I must say, he does look the best.

Did he tell you of who and what I was?
The practitioner with whom you were dealing?
Could you guess it from the story he told?
Were tiny details left out to save a hurt feeling?

My name is embedded in this town.
I'm baked in it through and through.
And you want me to give it back. Just like that?
But, to who? Who the hell are you?

Didn't you enjoy your new wealth?
Was it *not* the solution to *all* your problems?
But, sure. Yeah. I'll return the town to you.
On the condition; I like to leave things as I found 'em.

Has anyone here tasted the fruit in hand?
Has anyone taken a single bite?
Have you passed through doors that seemed familiar?
Try if you might. Just try if you might.

I told him if the pact gets broken
Every dream in this town would become awoken
Back to reality.
And a *darker* one at that.
I told your friend here, clear as day, 'Don't break the pact.'

MAN. We all take to kneeling to grab up some of that earth
to see what he's talking about. What looks like mineral
richness in palates of rainbow'd ochre... turn to dust
upon the slightest touch.

A scramble. Knees scraped from kissing the newly
rough land match *hands* made pricked and bloodied
by thorns on newly wild vines. How the tomatoes bite
back like rose stems? How the melons turn like cactus?
We bite into fruits that lost their juicy sweet, but leave
streams down the corners of our mouths the taste of
seawater.

[MUSIC NO. 11 – AM I A KING (REPRISE)]

SORRY COUNTRY ROAD
        SORRY COUNTRY ROAD THERE
        SORRY COUNTRY ROAD
                THAT LED TO US ONCE
YOU HAD TO BE PAVED OVER FOR SOMETHING NEW HERE
WHAT DID WE DO HERE?
WHAT DID I DO HERE?

Here come y'all racing to your homes to find nothing but painted flats like movie set dressing. Beautiful on the outside. Crossing thresholds into... emptiness. No relief. No ease. No peace. Just the fabrication of your every wish...

WHAT DID I DO HERE?

STRANGER. And as for you with your new-found wisdom
Your statue center of town
Did you think it wise to entice them?
You made a deal that could only let them down

You all remember not knowing his name
Before he lured you all into this mess?
Did you know *I* promised him a kingly station?
And in exchange for this town's *soul* no less.

He presented me with such melancholia
Oh, and said you all never lent a hand
But, take stock of what he just gave away
Now, take stock of this man who calls himself your friend

So, here is the town I return
One far emptier than it was before
And now with a man who had no qualms
About leading you right to Ruin's door...

And so, I think what I will take in exchange for all my investment
Time, effort and mental stress

Is taking pleasure in watching the tables turn
As I put you all to the test.

If you want *real* riches. The kind a *legacy* could extend, You all are going to have to figure out what you do about him

Sacrifice this one for the many. Send this sad little man back to the outskirts of town.

And I'll make your wealth a reality
You'll get far more than I promised *him*
A town more vibrant than you've ever dreamed

Or, he can stay here with you. Inside destruction and debris
The foul water. The salted ground. This sour air.
You'll have to rebuild on your own. From next to nothing.
With this withering man just... standing there.

So...

Have fun with that
I'm sure there's a hat
You all can pass around
You good people like voting
And that's fine with me
But your time is winding down

> *(The* **STRANGER** *hands a townsperson the letter. Maybe it comes from a pocket.)*

[MUSIC NO. 12 – THEN COME BACK AROUND (REPRISE)]

THEN COME BACK AROUND
THEN COME BACK AROUND
WE ALL COME BACK AROUND
TO THE EDGE OF THIS STREET

THEN COME BACK AROUND
THEN COME BACK AROUND
WE ALL COME BACK AROUND
TO THE EDGE OF THIS STREET

THEN COME BACK AROUND
THEN COME BACK AROUND
WE ALL COME BACK AROUND
TO THE EDGE OF THIS STREET

MAN.

THEN COME BACK AROUND
THEN COME BACK AROUND
WE ALL COME BACK AROUND
TO THE EDGE OF THIS STREET

(The **VOTE CONDUCTOR** *reads the letter as instructed. The* **TOWNSPEOPLE** *vote. The tally is announced. The* **MAN**'s *fate is sealed. Either way.)*

And I am grateful...

End

APPENDIX MATERIALS

I. Vote Conducting Script

*(A LITTLE NOTE: This is an example of how, when all things go as planned, the vote will unfold. It is recommended that there be a guide to facilitate the **AUDIENCE**'s participation. Expect variations, impromptu and unexpected interactions. This is the nature of participatory theater. Most importantly, be gentle and respectful to your audience volunteers. The messy, unpolished, anxiety driven, potential chaos of the moment is what makes it beautiful and moving. After this script you will find templates of all **AUDIENCE** materials as well as helpful material for recruiting your **VOTE CONDUCTOR**.)*

*(The **STRANGER** hands a **TOWNSPERSON** (the pre-chosen **AUDIENCE VOTE CONDUCTOR**) the letter. Perhaps it's in a gold envelope. The **AUDIENCE GUIDE** can position themselves in view of the **AUDIENCE VOTE CONDUCTOR** just as assurance to the **AUDIENCE MEMBER**. The **VOTE CONDUCTOR**, if following the written instructions on the letter, will stand and begin to speak the following.)*

AUDIENCE VOTE CONDUCTOR. This man has both negotiated and betrayed a contract in our name. And without our knowing. He has put us all at risk for his <u>personal</u> gain. As a result, we now live with foul water, a salted ground and sour air. Our homes are destroyed.

We must vote to either:

<u>Punish</u> this man for the crimes he has committed by sending him back to the outskirts of town and, in exchange, make our wealth a reality.

Or, <u>absolve</u> this man of his crimes and <u>keep him here</u> among us; knowing that we will be left with this destruction and must rebuild on our own from nothing.

Prepare yourselves to vote.

> (**VOTE CONDUCTOR** *sits as* **AUDIENCE GUIDE** *comes forward.*)

AUDIENCE GUIDE. May I have a community member willing to read the contents of this envelope.

> (*The* **GUIDE** *hands the* **BLUE NOTE** *to the volunteer to read.*)

May I have a community member willing to read the contents of *this* envelope.

> (*The* **GUIDE** *hands the* **RED NOTE** *to the volunteer to read and indicates for each* **VOLUNTEER** *to read contents.* **BLUE** *should be read first in all instances. The* **GUIDE** *should ask each* **VOLUNTEER** *to stand.*)

BLUE NOTE AUDIENCE MEMBER. *(They stand and read the following loud enough so that everyone in the room can hear.)* 'The greatness of a <u>community</u> is most accurately measured by the <u>compassionate</u> actions of its members. Never forget that justice is what <u>love</u> looks like in public.' (**AUDIENCE MEMBER** *repeats as instructed by the paper.*)

RED NOTE AUDIENCE MEMBER. *(They stand and read the following loud enough so that everyone in the room can hear.)* <u>Justice</u> has not been done until the guilty get the <u>punishment</u> they deserve. Punishment is the <u>tool</u> whereby the community protects the common good against the individual. (**AUDIENCE MEMBER** *repeats as instructed by the paper.*)

> (*Meanwhile the* **AUDIENCE GUIDE** *has handed the* **VOTE CONDUCTOR** *a second letter to read*

out-loud when the **RED** *and* **BLUE** *passages are complete. The* **VOTE CONDUCTOR** *stands.)*

VOTE CONDUCTOR. *(Reading.)* Now we vote on the fate of this community.

Ayes or nays.

<u>No half ways.</u>

*Understanding the consequences, if you vote to punish this man for his crimes, please raise your hand <u>now</u>.

> **(VOTE CONDUCTOR** *counts all raised hands out loud so everyone gathered can hear. The* **GUIDE** *will keep the tally.)*

> *(*This works well in groups under 100. If you have greater than 100 you may opt to alter the vote language above and instead call for a verbal vote of AYES. Ex: If you vote to punish this man for his crimes please say AYE now.)*

> *(Reading.)*

You may put your hands down. Thank you.

Understanding the consequences, if you vote to absolve this man of his crimes, please raise your hand now.

> **(VOTE CONDUCTOR** *counts all raised hands out loud so everyone gathered can hear.* **GUIDE** *will keep the Tally.)*

> *(Reading.)*

You may put your hands down. Thank you.

> *(The* **GUIDE** *reads the following and hands* **VOTE CONDUCTOR** *the resolution that corresponds with the vote results.)*

AUDIENCE GUIDE. The tally is:

_____ ABSOLVE to _____PUNISH

VOTE CONDUCTOR. *(Reading.)* The COMMUNITY has
    voted to:
    <u>Absolve</u> this man.
    He will stay here among us.
    We must rebuild from nothing.
    This <u>gathering</u> is concluded.

        (They sit.)

OR

        (Reading.)

The COMMUNITY has voted to:
<u>Punish</u> this man.
We will send him back to the outskirts of town.
And make our wealth a reality.
This gathering is concluded.

        (They sit.)

        (A bell rings.)

THE MAN. And I am Grateful.

        (THE MAN *exists. Blackout.)*

II. Getting your Audience Vote Conductor to Volunteer

(Select this person prior to the show beginning and make sure to get their explicit consent to participate. You'll want to designate a seat just off the aisle and located in a position that most of the audience can hear and see this person with little effort. It's best for the performer playing **MAN** *to have the same seat location to hand the envelope to each night. Or plan a way to let the performer know each night where the vote conductor is located. You'll want to have a backup seat location just in case your audience participant does not want to participate or the seat is unoccupied.)*

(The **AUDIENCE** *sample letter that the* **GUIDE***'s shows to the potential audience participant is included below.)*

Hi, my name is____

This seat has been designated as the community's Vote Conductor's seat. That means that at a certain point tonight a vote will be called and, with a little help from me, we would like for you conduct the vote.

You will be handed an envelope. In the envelope you'll find instructions that look like this:

(Hands them the **Sample Audience Letter** *and asks them to take as much time as they need to read it to themselves.)*

Just like it says here, we ask that you <u>read</u> out-loud all of the text in **bold** and do everything in (<u>parentheses</u>).

I will be right next to you when the time comes, in case you need me.

Will you be tonight's Vote Conductor?

(If the **AUDIENCE MEMBER** *does not want to* **VOLUNTEER,** *go on to next seat option.)*

III. Documents to Print and Distribute

> SAMPLE VOTE CONDUCTOR LETTER for audience member to review:

Dear Audience Member,

You have been chosen to conduct the vote. If you accept, you will be handed a letter in a gold envelope near the end of the event. Some of the letter's content will be in **bold** and some in (parenthesis).

Everything in (parenthesis) is an instruction just for you.

Everything in **bold** is for you to read out loud.

For example, your letter will look something like this:

> Dear Townsperson,
>
> (Please stand and speak loud enough for everyone to hear you)
>
> **We as a community have come together today to decide blah blah blah.**
> (Instructions just for you to do)
>
> **Please raise your hands if you vote to blah blah blah.**
> (More instructions just for you to do)
>
> **You may put your hand down. Thank you.**
> (Instructions, instructions, instructions)

Remember Everything in (parenthesis) is an instruction just for you. Everything in **bold** is for you to read out loud.

Will you accept this request to be our vote conductor?

> #1 Vote conductor letter to be placed in Golden Envelope

(This part is just for you to read to yourself.
Remember:

    Everything in (parentheses) is an instruction just for you.

    Everything in **bold** is for you to read out loud.

Ready. Here goes!

Please stand.

Please read loud enough so that everyone in the room can hear you.)

This man has both negotiated and betrayed a contract in our name and without our knowing.

He has put us all at risk for his <u>personal</u> gain.

As a result, we now live with foul water, a salted ground and sour air. Our homes are destroyed.

We must vote to either:

<u>Punish</u> this man for the crimes he has committed by <u>sending him back</u> to the outskirts of town and, in exchange, make our wealth a reality.

Or, <u>absolve</u> this man of his crimes and <u>keep him here</u> among us, knowing that we will be left with this destruction, and will have to rebuild on our own from nothing.

Prepare yourselves to vote.

(Your Guide will now give additional instructions. Meanwhile, you may sit.)

#2 Vote conductor letter read after Red and Blue passages

(Please stand and read the following loud enough so that everyone in the room can hear you.)

Now we vote on the fate of this community.
Ayes or nays.
<u>No half ways.</u>

Understanding the consequences, if you vote to **punish** this man for his crimes, please raise your hand **now**.

(Please count all raised hands out loud so everyone can hear you. Your guide will keep the tally.)

You may put your hands down. Thank you.

Understanding the consequences, if you vote to **absolve** this man of his crimes, please raise your hand **now**.

(Please count all raised hands out loud so everyone can hear you. Your guide will keep the tally.)

You may put your hands down. Thank you.

(Continue standing to pronounce the results.)

Guide Tally sheet

GUIDE:

The tally is:

_____ **ABSOLVE to** _____**PUNISH**

Community resolution

The COMMUNITY has voted to:
Absolve this man.
He will stay here among us.
We must rebuild from nothing.
This gathering is concluded.

      (You may sit.)

The COMMUNITY has voted to:
Punish this man.
We will send him back to the outskirts of town.
But make our wealth a reality.
This gathering is concluded.

(You may sit.)

Volunteer 'COMMUNITY' Passages

(Blue Passage.)

(Please stand and read the following loud enough so that everyone in the room can hear you.)

The <u>greatness</u> of a community is most accurately measured by the <u>compassionate</u> actions of its members.
Never forget that <u>justice</u> is what
<u>love</u> looks like in public.

(Please read the passage one more time out loud so that everyone can hear. Then you may sit.)

(Red Passage.)

(Please stand and read the following loud enough so that everyone in the room can hear you.)

<u>Justice</u> has not been done until the <u>guilty</u> get the punishment they deserve.
Punishment is the tool whereby the <u>community</u>
protects the common good against the <u>individual</u>.

(Please read the passage one more time out loud so that everyone can hear. Then you may sit.)